THE RAVENS OF FAIRBOURNE HALL

Book 3

For my boys, Che and Noah

CHAPTER 1

"I don't think we should be doing this Mythra."

"Oh, come on Tam, where is your sense of adventure?"

"Adventure! We just teleported to Egypt. Egypt!" Tam was feeling a bit stressed and Mythra could hear the strain in his voice. "We were lucky we didn't appear on top of the pyramid or half in and half out of a wall!"

"Look Tam, we made it. We appeared right outside the great pyramid just as we wanted and I wish you wouldn't keep on putting these scary images in my head," demanded Mythra. "You know our thoughts play a big role in teleporting. You really need to stop these thoughts otherwise one day they will happen."

"And now that we are inside the pyramid, none of our magical items are working," complained Tam.

"Well at least we were able to get past the guards and inside with no problem," retorted Mythra.

"Yes, but if anyone comes in we are in trouble. There is no way for us to escape," continued Tam.

"Then we need to be quiet and get on with it," said Mythra. "I have to admit, this is so exciting. I always wanted to come to the Great Pyramid. This place is totally awesome and I feel like I've been here before. Do you think that's possible Tam? Do you think I may have had a past life in ancient Egypt?"

"I suppose it is," said Tam grumpily. "Come on it's this way." Tam led the way past the steel gate that stops access to a long tunnel that descends down under the pyramid. "Wait a minute," said Tam. He took out his magical golden key and opened the padlock that locked the gate. The key was the first magical item they found after the fire at their home, Fairbourne Hall; the fire that had put their mother in the hospital in a coma whilst their father, Corvus Raven, was missing and presumed dead.

"What are you doing Tam," asked Mythra, "That's not the way. This magic map is showing that we need to go up to the King's Chamber, not down, below the pyramid."

"It's just in case," answered Tam, "I just had the feeling that it may be a useful thing to do. It may throw someone off our scent."

"You are a funny one Tammuz," said his sister, "You are so overly cautious I can hardly believe you're my twin." She grabbed the padlock and snapped it shut. She gave it a tug to make sure it was fully locked. "It could also signal to someone that there is someone here, so I think it stays locked," she insisted.

Since the fire they had been on the run from a mysterious organisation known as the Nyx. The Nyx were after the magic items kept hidden by their parents, items that had now fallen into the children's hands to protect.

They entered into the Grand Gallery, a long corridor that slopes steeply upwards and gets narrower and narrower above the children's heads.

"Look," said Mythra, "this is the granite plug." She was looking back down to the bottom of the corridor and the huge piece of stone that blocked the end of the corridor. "This massive piece of stone was used to block the passage and it fits perfectly. It's made of granite which is a really hard stone yet it's been shaped to fit perfectly in this space. To get past this granite plug explorers had to dig through the softer, limestone wall to the side of it. But just think, thousands of years ago when the pyramid was in use, this stone plug must have been up at the top end of this sloping corridor. They built the pyramid with this plug held at the top of this slope knowing that one day they would want to close this passage off and when that day came they released the plug and it slid all the way down here, fitting perfectly in place. Absolutely perfectly! And look at the size of it! It's huge!"

"I hadn't really thought about it but now that you mention it, that is pretty impressive. Quite amazing really," conceded Tam.

"Michael said that the Atlanteans came here and built this over 10 000 years ago. Thousands of years before the reign of King Khufu who many believe built it," continued Mythra. "He says that back then everyone was clairvoyant with super senses. People could see the gods and could do magic just by thinking about it."

"Yes, but they had no free will," interceded Tam. "They couldn't choose or question. They had to lose those psychic powers in order to gain the state of mind we have now. This slope is steep isn't it. It's a good job that there's this modern handrail to hold on to."

"Yes," said Mythra, "but we are nearly there. The next step for us is the King's chamber while the next step for human evolution is to regain the magical clairvoyant consciousness of the past while retaining our modern scientific way of thinking and our free will as to how we use our powers. Michael said that those ancient Atlanteans knew they were losing their psychic powers so they built places like this to help mankind to achieve the powers that had been normal in the past."

"An initiation centre, he called it," continued Tam.

Michael was a friend of their father's that had been helping them to avoid the Nyx. He understood which items the Nyx were most interested in obtaining and had agreed to help the children take hold of those items first.

They reached the top of the steeply sloping corridor and found the small opening to their left that leads to the King's chamber.

"In here," said Tam, "but we have to crawl through."

Mythra followed Tam, crawling through the low passage that leads into the chamber. They both stood and shone their torches around the room. Mythra gasped as she saw the smooth black walls for the first time.

"This is just amazing, she said. I so feel like I have been here before Tam. I almost want to cry and you know I'm not the crying type but this place … it just holds some kind of emotion for me that I can't explain."

"I think I kind of feel it too," said Tam. "I definitely feel something weird in here."

They both stood and stared ahead at the stone box in front of them.

"Look at the map," said Tam.

Mythra took the map from her pocket and opened it. It was the magic map that showed them where they needed to be. They shone their torches on to the map and saw there a picture of the stone box inside this very room, easily recognisable with one corner slightly damaged.

"Well, this is where we are meant to be," said Mythra.

Tam walked over to the stone box. "So," he said, "this is where the ancient kings were initiated, where they had their psychic powers turned on, lying in this box. And the Sibylline books are supposed to be here?" He asked as he put one foot in the stone box and then the other and then lowered himself into the box as if getting in to the bath.

The Sibylline books were written in ancient Egypt, many thousands of years ago. They record the positions of the stars through the ages and years into the future. Through understanding the stars, the Egyptians understood the story of man and knew exactly what should happen and when. Now they were the number one target of the Nyx because they allowed the possibility of time travel.

"What are you doing?" Asked Mythra.

"Erm, I don't know," replied Tam. "I hadn't really thought about it. I think I've been on auto pilot. Lying in the box just seemed like the right thing to do so I did and I just had an idea. I was wondering how we are going to find these books without any of our magical items working and it seems to me that sound has been pretty important in using these items so maybe if we find the right sound they might just appear in front of us. Hold on."

Tam took his phone out of his pocket. It had a sonogram app which could produce any tone. He pressed the button on his phone and then pressed it again.

"Oh no," he said, "my phone isn't working."

Mythra took hers from her pocket. "That's funny, she said, neither is mine. It's as if the battery is dead."

Tam cleared his throat and said, "Okay, we'll just have to do this the old-fashioned way."

As he lay in the box he began to vocalise. He sang a long 'O', starting at a very deep tone and slowly raising the pitch. He stopped for a deep breath and continued and then breathed and continued once more. Eventually he lifted his head from the box and looked around.

"Nothing?" He asked.

"No, I can't see anything," said Mythra, "although the acoustics in here are amazing. I can feel the sound vibrating through my body and it makes my eyes go all wobbly."

"Well, you should try being in here," said Tam. "It's as if this box is the sound focal point of the room. It's as if all the sound I'm producing is bouncing around the room and then focusing back at the box. The box itself feels as if its vibrating around me, which is impossible as it's made from very hard granite stone."

It was by singing in this way that they had first discovered the magic key that worked in any lock. Objects covered in a special substance called monatomic gold or Ormus powder could be phased slightly out of time and so become invisible by finding the correct musical key. Objects hidden in this way could be recovered by again producing the right note. Objects covered in this special ash of gold could also be made to float by warming them or to sink through the earth by cooling them. Ancient Egyptians called this special gold dust, 'Tcham'.

"Let me have a go then," said Mythra.

Tam climbed out of the box and Mythra climbed in and lay down. She breathed deep and then emitted a deep 'O' sound just as Tam had. Slowly she let the sound raise to a higher pitch and then she stopped for a deep breath and continued once more just as Tam had. Eventually she stopped and popped her head up with a huge grin on her face. "That was incredible," she said. "The box really does vibrate as you said. Any sign of the book?"

"Nothing," said Tam, "but I see what you mean. My eyes went all wobbly as well while you were doing that. I have never known a room like this."

"But no magic book," said Mythra, disappointed as she sat up. "Let's look at the map," she said. She took the magic map from her pocket and opened it out. Tam came closer and looked with his torch also. The map showed the stone box in which Mythra sat but quickly started to move back away from the box. Within moments the map showed the pyramid from the outside and continued to zoom out as if it were flying backwards away from the pyramid at great speed. Again, the scene shifted to something looking more like a map. They could make out the Nile and North-East Africa and then the map moved and changed. They saw Europe and then Britain and then the very North of the British-isles. Above Britain the map showed a group of tiny islands.

"Is that the Orkneys?" Asked Tam.

"It looks like it is. Come on we have to get out of here to teleport back to Britain," said Mythra.

"Okay, but I don't understand," said Tam, "I thought we were here for the books. This magic map is supposed to show us where we are meant to be. If we are not here for the books then why did we need to come here?"

"I don't know Tam but I have always wanted to come here and I feel I am meant to be here and that I have been here before. I was just thinking about what Michael said about how in the past the ancient kings underwent a resurrection initiation here. He said they would pass over into death and then return back to life and this would empower them and allow them to be the king."

"So, it was also like their coronation ceremony," added Tam.

"Yes, I guess so," said Mythra, "but the thing is, what I just realised, is that we are both named after gods of resurrection. Mythra is the Roman god and Tammuz is Sumerian or Mesopotamian isn't it?"

"Yes, so, what are you saying? We were just always meant to come here? That this is some kind of initiation?" asked Tam.

"Maybe," answered Mythra. "Perhaps we just accidentally initiated ourselves."

"So, does that mean we have to die and return now?" asked Tam.

"Like Harry Potter," laughed Mythra.

"Or Aragorn," said Tam.

"Aragorn doesn't die in the Lord of the Rings," complained Mythra.

"No, but he travels to the land of the dead and raises an army of the dead in order to become the King of men, doesn't he? Explained Tam.

"Yes, I suppose you are right," said Mythra, "I wonder if Tolkien was an initiate?"

The children crawled back through the little corridor to the Grand Gallery and descended the steep incline. Once more they reached the massive granite plug that blocked the end of the passageway and the tunnel that goes around this obstacle. Carefully and quietly they made their way around the blockage. Mythra was in the lead. Suddenly she stopped and held up her hand. She looked at Tam and put her fingers to her lips indicating that Tam needed to be quiet. Both the children listened intently. There were voices up ahead. Three Egyptian guards were accompanied by two agents of the Nyx had entered the Pyramid by the only entrance. The children were trapped.

CHAPTER 2

From the Journal of Corvus Raven

21 April 2001

It has now been one year since I left the secret valley of the enlightened masters. I have found life just as difficult as my master predicted since leaving there. At times I find myself sinking into hatred towards my fellow human beings which is strange to me after years of not knowing such an emotion. I thought I was cured of hateful thoughts and feelings. However, I find people perplexing and frustrating and frankly, quite stupid. I remember my master joking with me one day. He said that "to an unenlightened man the world is nothing but suffering and to the enlightened man the world is insufferable". Now I understand what he meant. I find that I must meditate for long periods each day just to retain my own sanity and to retain only the smallest amount of the powers I had when I returned to life a year ago.

However, I have made progress in my mission. I have been working as a security guard in the British Museum, under the name of Frasier Moleford, for the past six months. I have my old friend Michael to thank for the false documents that have allowed me to hide my true identity.

For months I have been aware of the comings and goings of politicians and military personnel and their interest in certain items in the museum. I am surprised at how loosely they talk in front of us lowly guards. They probably think we are too stupid to understand what they are talking about. Also, I get the impression that they could make us forget anything that we see or hear that they do not wish us to. There have been a number of occasions when guards have accompanied items to private viewings but do not seem to remember anything about these evenings when I ask. In order to better understand what is going on; which items are being used, which are hidden and which are sought after, I have been researching magical objects in my spare time. Largely I have to look to the world of myth and legend as there is no inventory of magical items to view in a world that does not believe in magic.

Recently I have come across an object called the Chintamani stone, which is said to have fell from the sky thousands of years ago. Apparently, this stone can be used to control the will and thoughts of men. Could it be that this stone is being used to make my fellow guards forget what they have seen?

Finally, I seem to have come to the attention of some of those people that I find most suspicious, those who I believe are involved in the procurement and use of magical items. I have been asked to accompany a group of guards at a private function at which certain items will be viewed.

Furthermore, I have heard a name for the secretive group who I believe are the stealers and users of these items. I overheard the name Nyx, which I believe is a Greek goddess of night, which is appropriate for those who wish to keep us in the dark.

CHAPTER 3

Mythra and Tam looked at each other in panic, not knowing what to do. The Nyx and the Guards made their way through the entrance tunnel and approached the granite plug of the Grand Gallery. Just before they reached the plug and the entrance to the Grand Gallery they stopped by the beginning of the other tunnel that descends down under the pyramid, the tunnel blocked by a locked gate.

The children heard the agents of the Nyx speaking in English. "Look, one of them said, this padlock has been opened, the gates aren't locked."

Mythra and Tam looked at each other confused, knowing that the padlock was definitely locked.

"What was that noise?" asked the other. "There is someone down there. Come on." All five men quickly descended down into the depths below the pyramid by the light of their torches.

Mythra peeped her head out from the entrance to the Grand Gallery. The tunnel was clear. All the men were gone. She signalled for Tam to follow quietly and they tiptoed past the entrance to the descending tunnel and on towards the entrance to the pyramid. Mythra glanced at the padlock and shook her head. She knew she had locked it so how was it open?

It was night outside so no light guided their way and they turned off their torches in case anyone was outside. In the dark they groped their way forward, slowly and quietly.

At the entrance way they smelled fresh night air and felt a slight breeze against their faces as they poked their heads through the opening and looked around. Below them, down on the ground were men. They looked like Egyptian guards, with guns.

The children crouched in the shadows of the entranceway and decided that they needed to attempt to teleport from this spot. They held hands and thought of Michael and his living room. Tam pressed a button on his phone which was now working perfectly and the sonogram app started to produce a low-pitched noise that gradually rose to a higher and higher note.

The guards on the ground heard the noise and became agitated. Men started to climb the great stone blocks of the pyramid towards them, wondering where the noise was coming from. Tam and Mythra concentrated hard, determined not to be distracted by the movement and noise headed their way. The noise of the sonogram rose higher and higher and then there was a flash.

CHAPTER 4

From the Journal of Corvus Raven

23 April 2001

What an amazing night!

I was asked to guard some extremely rare items at a private function at a very large house out in the countryside in the middle of Essex. There were a number of very rich and powerful people present, many of whom I recognised from the military, the media and the world of politics.

I was accompanying a number of items from the British Museum, one of which is a very interesting item called an Archimedes clock. However, there were a number of other items on display from private collections. One was a sword labelled the sword of truth. There were also some articles of clothing that were said to be made from the Golden Fleece and some stones said to have been made from the original Chintamani stone. These blue stones had been fashioned into a necklace and a pair of matching earrings.

All evening I tried my best to eavesdrop on conversations in order to divine the purpose of these meetings of the rich and powerful and it seems to me that these occasions have a number of purposes. First, items are bought and sold. Some items need to be copied so that the original can be replaced without anyone knowing so there is talk of the cost of specialist artisans and their ability to fool experts in this matter.

Some objects just seemed to be on display, maybe as a show of power. The stones of Chintamani seemed to be owned by one of the men who fund one of Britain's largest political parties.

Some of the items, it seems, were there to be checked out for authenticity. I gathered that some objects were difficult to use or needed to be used in combination with other items and so it isn't always possible to know if an item is genuine or not. To help in this matter there were a number of people present who were referred to as psychics. These people had time with the objects in order to determine whether the object was truly magical and if so how should it be used. I gathered that these psychics, although highly revered, are not always reliable. I wondered at my own ability to determine the use of these objects. I cannot wait to try.

Some of these psychics did give me a second look, as if suspecting that I was not all I seemed. However, due to years of meditation I am used to keeping a completely quiet mind in the company of telepaths. Tonight, I am proud to say that I was able to go even further in this deception as I was able to broadcast extremely boring and normal thoughts about what was on the television and about the varying fortunes of a particular football club. After all, a security guard who is trained to keep his thoughts completely private may well arouse more suspicion than one who thinks normal 'British man' thoughts.

All of this was interesting enough for one night. I felt I had really made a good headway in my god given mission and great inroads into the shadowy world of the Nyx. However, there was more; an incident that made this night truly remarkable.

CHAPTER 5

The children opened their eyes and found themselves back in Michael's house. They were stood in his living room. They looked around. Michael was asleep on the sofa, snoring gently.

"Teleporting seems to be getting easier," said Mythra.

"Thank God for that," said Tam. "That was so cool." Both children looked at each other and smiled.

The next morning the children related the tale of their time in the Great Pyramid to Michael. "It sounds as if you were very lucky," he commented when he heard about their narrow escape. "The Nyx must have psychics on the lookout for you 24 hours a day!"

"But how did the Nyx agents get to Egypt so fast?" asked Tam.

"There are always Nyx agents posted at the Great Pyramid," answered Michael. "It is one of the earth's greatest initiation sites so it is monitored constantly. Anyone like you will get there at some point. And people like you are always of interest to the Nyx."

"People like us?" asked Mythra.

"Well, yes, or like your dad, or me. People who are interested in this kind of stuff and people who are in the process of waking up to the truth of a greater reality," went on Michael. "The Nyx tries to spot these people and co-opt them to their cause, or remove them from the game. I have heard reports of such people being locked up and studied so that the Nyx can try to artificially induce powers in people."

"But why were we sent there by the map?" asked Tam. "Oh no," he gasped, "I just thought. Maybe the Sibylline books appeared down in the lower room below the pyramid. Maybe that's what the Nyx heard down there. Maybe they have the books already!"

"I suppose that is possible," concluded Michael. "However, it's probably best not to jump to conclusions. Maybe the books just weren't there. Maybe there was another reason for your being sent to the Great Pyramid. I've been thinking, he continued, remember that I said that you needed to find the etheric box of the Atlanteans? Well listening to your description of being in the king's chamber, lying in that stone box, with waves of sound washing over you and through you, it brought that etheric box to my mind. Perhaps that stone box is the etheric box? Perhaps you have prepared yourself for time travel without even knowing it? And if that is true, then it suggests to me that it will happen, you will find the books. Why else would you need to be prepared?"

The children sat with their mouths gaping open, digesting the enormity of this news and understanding that there did seem to be some sense in this analysis. Realising this perked their spirits and made them feel positive about the future.

"Oh, I have some good news," continued Michael, "well, it's sort of good. Let me explain." He pulled out a mirror just larger than a man's hand. "This," he said, "is a magic mirror. There are in fact two of them. A pair of mirrors. Now, the thing is, you can look into one mirror, that is this one, and see through the other mirror no matter where it is."

"So where is the other mirror?" asked Mythra.

"Ah, yes now that is a very good question. In fact, that is exactly the question you needed to ask. Well, as it happens, you know I took a photograph of you two a few days ago, well, I developed the photo and placed it in front of the mirror and sent that to the hospital where you mother is in a coma. I phoned the hospital this morning and the nurse said that they had received the photo and put it next to her bed."

"So, we can see through it? We can see mom in the hospital?" asked Tam frantically.

"Yes of course, that is the whole idea," said Michael, "let me show you how. Now just look into the mirror with full concentration and start that sonogram phone app thingy and that should do it."

"Wont the picture block our view?" asked Mythra.

"No, no, not at all," answered Michael. "Actually, having your picture over the mirror acts as a kind of magical lock so that only you can see through the other side. Now I shall give you two some privacy and leave you to it. Don't go upsetting yourselves now. The nurse said that your mother is doing fine, there is no long-term damage. In fact, they said there is no reason why she shouldn't soon wake. Anyway, I will leave you for a bit."

With that Michael left the room and the children spent some time looking in on their mother whom they could not go and visit in person due to the danger of being found by the Nyx.

CHAPTER 6

From the Journal of Corvus Raven

As I watched the crowd of gathered guests I found one of the guests watching me. It was a woman and I couldn't help but feel that I recognised her but could not remember from where.

I feared for a while that she was a Nyx psychic that had uncovered my ruse and who was about to blow my cover. Whenever I looked around, there she was staring at me. When she saw me looking at her she quickly turned away.

All evening I wracked my brains trying to remember where I had seen her before and then it came to me. She was a regular at the British Museum. However, she always seemed to come alone. She was never in the company of those people whom I suspected were part of the Nyx although that could have been a possibility.

As the evening drew on, one of my colleagues relieved me of my position on the stairs where I had an excellent view of the crowds of people below. At this time, I was allowed 10 minutes break before taking up a new position, wandering the display rooms upstairs. During my break I visited the toilet. Upon leaving the room on the upper floor, I walked out to see this lady before me. She was about to enter the lady's toilet nearby.

However, in that moment we were closer to each other than we had been all evening. Our eyes instantly met and I was transfixed. I could not look away and I believe that she felt the same. Everything changed in that moment. Her face seemed to glow and float independently of her body. Her body merged with the background which seemed to be no more than a painting made of dots and broad brushstrokes. The air between us seemed to shimmer and move. I felt that, although we both stood completely frozen still, we were both on conveyer belts that were bringing us closer together and we zoomed towards one another. I felt almost dizzy, as if I were about to fall over or faint.

Then just as suddenly, we heard people coming up the stairs and the spell was broken. She looked slightly embarrassed and entered the women's toilets. I had to suddenly move my feet to stop myself from falling forwards as my vision returned to normal.

CHAPTER 7

Sometime later the children sat with Michael looking at the magic map. "Yes," said Michael, "that is definitely the Orkney isles. In fact, that is the main island and if I'm not mistaken that point on the map is Maeshowe."

"What's a Maeshowe?" asked Mythra.

"Well, it's an ancient chamber, my dear. Have you not heard of it?" asked Michael. "It's many thousands of years old. It is called a burial chamber just as the pyramids are called tombs but of course, no bodies were ever found there, either at Maeshowe or in the pyramids. It's another initiation site, of course, used many thousands of years ago as a way of helping people awake to the magic of the world. There are many such places around the world.

Anyway, Maeshowe is a bit like a mini pyramid, like a little hill. Let me show you on the computer."

Michael tapped on the keys of his computer and in moments pictures of a small green mound appeared surrounded by a circular wall. He clicked through some pages and showed the children pictures of the tunnels within and the vaulted chamber in the middle.

"I can see the similarity with the Great Pyramid," said Mythra. "These tunnels are just like the ones in the pyramid and this room in the middle is a bit like the Grand Gallery, the way the walls close in as they go up so forming the roof."

"Yes, that's right," said Michael. "Each slab of stone slightly overhangs the one below and so a large domed roof is formed. Sunlight shines down these tunnels at a particular time of year. Thousands of years ago that would have been at mid-winter, as that is when the sun is said to come back to life, just as an initiate comes back to life due to the ceremonies that took place here. Also, this a perfect sound chamber, just like the Great Pyramid it has perfect acoustics. Remember what it was like lying in the stone box? Well, this room will give you a similar feeling as it is also harmonically perfect."

Mythra pointed to some other pictures on the computer. "And what are these?" she asked.

"These are nearby standing stones, kind off similar to Stonehenge, aren't they?" explained Michael. "This are called the Ring of Brodgar."

"Wow," said Tam, "they are pretty impressive. Looks like we are going to the Orkneys. Do they have Nyx agents stationed there also?"

"Probably not," answered Michael reassuringly. "Which is why your father may have hidden the books there. However, they can get there pretty quickly once they know you are there so you won't have time for sightseeing. Just get the books and get out."

"Okay, then we go tonight," said Mythra, sounding more confident than she felt.

The children spent the day relaxing, eating and soaking up knowledge of Maeshowe and the surrounding area. By evening they felt they knew the Orkneys like the backs of their hands. They dressed up warm knowing that it would be cold so far north although it was normal for them to go out on missions with the golden fleece coat, hat, scarf, gloves and socks anyway but they thought it may help to have an extra layer.

Finally, they were ready to go.

"Be careful," said Michael.

CHAPTER 8

From the Journal of Corvus Raven

I returned to my duties, patrolling the upper display rooms, making a mental note of the items on display whilst trying to hide these thoughts from the psychics who were busy trying to tune into various objects.

Eventually, everyone was called down to dinner and I was left alone guarding one particular room. I knew that a camera sat high up in one corner of the room so I could not attempt to take any objects but at this stage that is not the plan. For now, I am content to watch and learn.

Suddenly the door opened but no-one entered. Perhaps it is the wind, I thought. I walked over to the door to see if anyone was outside of it. As I did so I felt something move past me. If I had not been sensitive to aura's I would have felt nothing but I felt this aura pass me.

My ability to see auras had greatly diminished since leaving the secret valley but thanks to regular meditation I am able to tune into auras with some effort when it is my will to do so.

I calmed my breathing, closed my eyes and found my own third eye; the glowing ball in the triangle that I had found a year before when I had returned from death. Once I had found the glowing ball I opened my eyes. The ball was still visible to me and it scanned the room before me. Almost instantly it found an aura that it latched onto. It scanned the aura and revealed it to be the size and shape of a person. I followed the aura as it moved silently away from me. Ahead of me there were a few pillars which provided some shielding from the watching camera. The aura must have known I was following as it quickly disappeared behind one of the pillars. Cautiously I followed. Then I felt a pinprick on my hand. I looked at my hand. There was a tiny dot of blood. Then the world span and I fell into darkness.

CHAPTER 9

The children had already decided on the exact location of arrival in the Orkneys and had studied the photos of the area. They knew they were ready. Tam pressed the button on his phone app. The noise began as a deep hum and rose in pitch and then a glow and the children disappeared from Michaels lounge. "Good luck," he said as he sat on his own.

At that moment the children appeared hundreds of miles away just outside the small hill called Maeshowe on mainland Orkney. The wind howled and the rain lashed down and the children were instantly chilled to the bone. It was pitch dark and the children took a moment to get their bearings and understand exactly where they were. They soon realised that the little hillock before them is where they needed to go and rushed towards it.

Within minutes they had found the entrance way. A locked gate barred their way but this was soon bypassed using the magic golden key.

"Oh, thank God I'm out of that weather," said Tam as they entered the dry, dark tunnel that led inside the hill. They felt safe enough to turn their torches on and slightly stooping made their way forward.

They were soon in the heart of the hill, inside the domed room built many thousands of years ago. Ancient runic symbols could be seen drawn here and there as they flashed their torches around.

"It's so still here," observed Mythra.

"Yes," agreed Tam, "now that you mention it, it is. My head is so silent. I didn't realise that normally my head is full of thoughts, constant chatter and I don't even notice it until it's turned off and then the silence is quite stunning."

"Yes," said Mythra, "it's like when the washing machine is on and you get used to the noise in the background and then you don't even notice it's on until it stops and then you notice the absence of noise."

Both of the children took a minute to just breathe silently, enjoying the complete lack of thinking in their heads.

Eventually Mythra spoke. "Come on, we must get on with it. Let's find those books."

Tam pulled out his phone to activate the sonogram app but Mythra stopped him. "Maybe it's this hat of knowing," she said, "but I don't want to do it that way. Come and sit with me."

CHAPTER 10

From the Journal of Corvus Raven

I felt something soft and warm pressed against my lips and became aware of my breathing. I opened my eyes and the light flooding in blinded me. As my eyes adjusted to the light I felt a hand holding my right arm down to the floor. I tried to move but I couldn't. I felt paralysed.

CHAPTER 11

They sat in the centre of the room. "Remember the Great Pyramid?" She asked. "We didn't use the sonogram there, did we. We just knew what to do. That's what we need to do here."

They breathed deeply for a minute or two and then Mythra began to sound out the letter 'o', elongated, loud and proud. She came to the end of the breath and as she began again Tam joined in with her. Together they sang, loud and low, breathing deeply in between, enjoying the silence.

Suddenly they both felt the need to stop. They sat with their eyes closed, in darkness and silence. Then they began to see images in their minds. Images like dream pictures appeared and they both watched. They saw standing stones, tall and smooth, almost sharp as knives slicing the night air which shimmered with purple and red. A Raven landed on the floor in front of the stone and called out a loud caw and another and another, each louder and longer as the stone vibrated and shook at the sound. The stone shook so fast that it almost disappeared as it seemed to become one with the shimmering purple air.

Then the Raven suddenly took off and flew to the west, towards the setting sun. Small houses appeared near the coast, houses that seemed to be in the ground. The raven landed in the most central room of the little group of houses. It walked to what looked like a chimney and cawed. A book dropped from the chimney and fell open in front of the raven who started to read. In the book was a picture of Gideon but this Gideon had little wings and a halo around his head. His hands were outstretched towards them and he was saying, "I am here to help you."

Then both of the children opened their eyes. The vision had

stopped and it was time to move. In unison they stood up and turned towards the entrance tunnel.

CHAPTER 12

From the Journal of Corvus Raven

Quickly now my vision began to clear. I looked up at a face looking down at me. It was a beautiful face. In that moment, to me, it looked like the face of an angel, a face that glowed with inner warmth, gentleness and beauty. It was the face of the lady who had been watching me all night, the lady I had seen outside the toilets. I knew I was still drugged and drowsy but I just didn't care. I smiled and she said, "I can see that you are a good man. Be careful who you work for."

CHAPTER 13

"Those stones," said Tam, "do you think that was the Ring of Brodgar or the Stones of Stenness? Both are here on the mainland and the stones look very similar."

"Maybe it's the hat, or maybe it's this room," answered Mythra, "but I am sure it's the Ring of Brodgar. And the little houses must be…"

"Skara Brae," finished Tam. "The ancient houses unearthed by archaeologists that are partially underground out on the west coast. The Ring of Brodgar is on the way. We have to head south to the Stones of Stenness and then north west between the Lock of Harray and the loch of Stenness. That way takes us straight on to the Ring of Brodgar and then we can carry on up the same way to Skara Brae."

"Well it's a good job we have our running shoes on then," said Mythra smiling. The truth was that they had their magic socks which allowed them to run incredibly fast.

"Do you think we can go fast enough to dodge the rain?" asked Tam.

"No," said Mythra. "I think we are going to get very wet."

CHAPTER 14

From the Journal of Corvus Raven

There was a humming sound and the angelic lady seemed to just vanish before me. It took a few minutes for me to be able to move. I stood slowly and looked around. One of the glass cases was open and an object was missing. It took me a minute to remember what had been there. It was the Chintamani jewellery.

CHAPTER 15

The children soon found themselves at the beautiful standing stones of Stenness. "These stones are so awesome," commented Mythra, "I wish I could spend more time here, and on a sunnier day, but these are definitely not the stones from the vision."

The children found the sharp turn to the right that led them between the lochs and quickly made their way to the Ring of Brodgar.

"This is definitely the place," said Tam, "and look, this is the stone from the vision. I have no doubt at all. It's the most westerly stone and I can almost feel the energy crackling around it."

"So," said Mythra, "I suppose we have to sing to it, just like the Raven in the vision."

"Yes, lets do this. I am soaked," complained Tam.

The children stood together before the stone and breathing deeply, they began, once more, to sing, just as they had in the pyramid and as they had in Maeshowe. They sang a long deep 'O'. The air around the stone shimmered and crackled with purple and red as if electricity were coming from the stone. The stone itself seemed to change colours and shimmer and vibrate. The children sang and sang and as their song became more intense the stone seemed to glow and became almost see through as if it were going to disappear into the purple buzzing sky. Suddenly there was a flash and the children knew that it was done. They both said, "thank you," as one to the stone and then turned and ran toward Skara Brae.

CHAPTER 16

From the Journal of Corvus Raven

I had no choice but to raise the alarm but I wanted the mystery woman to escape. I felt fine but pretended to be groggy and dizzy in order to give her more time. Instead of moving towards the emergency alarm button I staggered slowly towards the door. I opened the door and shouted but it was a quiet, slurred and feeble shout. I pretended to fall over and drag myself up again and then staggered into the hall. A guard was walking up the stairs and he saw me. He rushed to my aid and held me, asking me what had happened. I had given her all the time I could. I hoped she had escaped. I explained everything that had happened in as slow and slurred a way as possible and my fellow guard raised the alarm.

CHAPTER 17

The children soon reached the small ancient village overlooking the western sea. As the children stopped running and looked over the partially hidden ruins they realised that it had stopped raining. They stepped down into the well preserved little houses and followed the maze of passageways towards the central dwelling.

Finally, they came out of a small passage to find themselves in the central chamber.

"There is no chimney," said Tam.

"No, but that is definitely the hearth," said Mythra pointing to the spot where fires were obviously lit thousands of years before.

"There's nothing here," said Tam.

"I suppose we must sing once more," said Mythra.

The children held hands and breathed deep and once more they sang but this time with a strong determination. The end was in sight and they would not give up and they would not stop. This had to be done, now!

They sang and as they did so the ancient hearth began to glow and shimmer. They sang and sang and the glowing shimmer became more and more solid until suddenly it had become a solid object and the children, in shock, stopped.

Before them, in the ancient hearth sat a bag that shimmered like a film of oil on water in multicolours. It had a strap for putting over the shoulder and a flap to hide the contents inside. The children bent over towards the bag. They wanted to open it and see what was inside. They wanted to pull out the magical book that it contained.

Suddenly there was a noise, loud, chopping, whirring, breaking through the silence. The children looked up and were hit with a light that was blinding. There was another noise, an electrical crash and blue-white lightning.

Dazzled, Mythra grabbed the bag and pulled on Tam's arm. Together they climbed onto the low walls of the old village houses and tried to crawl away from the light and noise. They felt the force of wind almost blowing them over.

"It's a helicopter," shouted Tam as he turned to look at the source of the deafening noise and the blinding light. He turned away and followed Mythra as they crawled over the tops of walls away from light. Eventually they were clear of the old houses and reached level grassy ground.

"Run," shouted Mythra.

CHAPTER 18

From the Journal of Corvus Raven

I spent the next few hours being questioned by some of the very important people at the meeting. Thankfully, the recording from the camera in the room backed up what I said. The camera recorded the door opening but no-one coming through. It recorded me following nothing and then suddenly falling behind a pillar where I could not be seen, apart from my feet sticking out. A few minutes later I staggered to my feet. In the time I was unconscious, the glass case opened by itself, the blue stoned jewellery floated through the air to the pillars where I lay. They disappeared behind the pillars but were not seen again. Just before I stood up, the door once more opened by itself and then closed.

What really confused the very important people was the fact that I followed an invisible person across the room. I was asked what I thought had happened when the door opened. I said that maybe it was ghost that had entered the room. I was asked, what had I been following as there was nothing to see so I said I could hear footsteps. This caused some consternation amongst the assembled very important people. Saying that I thought I was following the footsteps of a ghost did not seem very believable.

There were psychics in the room with them during the questioning and it was hard work to not even think about the truth. The look on the faces of the psychics suggested that they did not believe me. Despite the evidence from the camera, it looked like I was going to be in trouble. This could be the end of my involvement with the Nyx.

Then I had a brainwave. Tell the truth! Well, part of it anyway. So, I admitted that I was covering something up, something that

I didn't want to tell because it was embarrassing, something that could stop me from being employed if people knew, something that might make people think I was a little bit crazy. I admitted that I could see auras.

I didn't quite say it like that. I spoke of moving air, of glowing light, of a sense and a feeling. I spoke of how it had always been this way for me, from an early age and how no-one understood this. In fact, I told them, people had treated me badly, as if I were crazy.

I told a partial truth but wrapped it up in words that elicited sympathy, especially from the psychics who nodded in reverent agreement because they knew how it felt to be misunderstood for having powers that made you different.

Everyone understood why I wouldn't admit to such a thing. But by admitting to being secretly psychic I just made myself a lot more useful. Security guards are two a penny. There was no guarantee I would ever be invited to one of these magic object events again. However, as a psychic I had just made sure I would be in the thick of things, deeply embedded with the Nyx, from now on.

CHAPTER 19

The children both ran as fast as they could, which is pretty fast when wearing magic socks, towards the south. Within moments they were far enough away from the helicopter to stop.

"What a noise," said Tam. "That was a helicopter. It must have been the Nyx. They are on to us."

"Let's teleport out while we can," said Mythra.

Tam took his phone from his pocket and tried to turn it on but nothing happened. "My phones not working," he said.

Mythra tried the small button on her coat that would activate the sound that would make her invisible but nothing happened. "My button is not working," she said. "I think that flash was some kind of E.M.P."

"What's an E.M.P.?" asked Tam.

"An electro-magnetic pulse," said Mythra. "It can disable electrical devices. I think that flash and crash was some kind of E.M.P. The helicopter must have been shielded in some way."

"So, we can't teleport out?" asked Tam.

"Not unless we can find the right frequency with our voices," replied Mythra.

"That's going to be difficult if we are concentrating on location at the same time," pointed out Tam.

"We should try," said Mythra.

The children tried to settle themselves and breath deeply when suddenly they were hit by a light and again they were affronted by a deafening noise.

"It's another helicopter," said Tam. "Run."

CHAPTER 20

From the Journal of Corvus Raven

11 May 2001

A few weeks later I was back at work in the museum. I was looking more deeply into the objects in the museum. I had realised that psychic powers were useful in identifying magical objects and understanding how they work. It is possible that there are many magic items in the museum that have yet to be found, that go unidentified. It was useful for me to practice tuning into objects so that I could be more useful to the Nyx, so I could gain their trust and so fulfil my mission. However, I had no magic objects of my own and was desperately waiting to be invited to work at another event, if for no other reason than having an opportunity to practice with real magic items.

I was staring deeply into a Greek shield but could find nothing special about it at all, when I heard a voice behind me.

"Hello sleeping beauty," she said, "please don't turn around. Have you found anything interesting in that shield?"

"Only your reflection," I replied.

"Maybe that's for the best, after all I may be Medusa. I may turn you to stone next time." She laughed. I wanted to turn and look at her but I found I could not. Her request that I do not turn had been a magical order which I could not resist.

"I could help you," I said, "I may be on your side."

"Now that is an interesting proposal," she said. "Perhaps we can discuss that on Friday evening. You will be free to move in one minute."

With those words she was gone.

CHAPTER 21

Again, the children ran as fast as they could to the south. Again, they stopped when away from the helicopter and tried to settle themselves but before they could try to concentrate on teleporting another helicopter appeared. Once more they were hit with light and sound. With no way to concentrate the children ran once more. They ran and ran until they reached a town on the south coast called Stromness. They found themselves running through the town until they could run no more. They were at the coast where houses surrounded the bay. A jetty ran out into the water and boats bobbed in the water on either side of it. The children paused, not knowing what to do. Suddenly a voice rang out.

"Tam, Mythra, here, this way." The children looked down the length of the jetty to see a figure standing in a boat, waving at them. "Come on. Quickly," they heard him shout.

"It's Gideon," said Tam. "Come on."

"No, wait," said Mythra. "How can he be here? I don't trust him."

"But we saw him in the book, in the vision," said Tam. "He is here to help us, remember? He saved us at the museum and you wanted to go back for him."

"Yes, I know but I'm not sure," protested Mythra. "How can he be here? It's the Orkneys. He can't just happen to be in the Orkneys. It has to be a trap."

"Listen," said Tam. "Hear that? That's helicopters. They are heading this way, now. We have no choice. We have to try this. This is no time for you to suddenly start being cautious. Come on."

Mythra sighed and resigned herself to Tam's logic. They had no choice. They ran down the jetty to the boat. Gideon stood on deck shouting, "Come on, hurry."

CHAPTER 22

From the Journal of Corvus Raven

12 May 2001

I have been invited to work at another event at the end of the week. On Friday night.

15 May 2001

Once more I find myself at a very large house in the country. Once more the house is full of very important people and a lot of rare objects in glass cases. However, this time when I had the opportunity, I studied the objects on display with much greater care. I found myself drawn to a sword, called the sword of truth.

After a little deep breathing and tuning into my third eye I found that this object glowed much more brightly than any objects that I had been studying in the museum. Other golden swords may well have a natural golden aura, a golden glow around them. At first glance this sword was no different but on closer inspection I found a green flame swirling around this sword as if two snakes coiled around it in constant motion.

Once more I closed my eyes and turned inward. The glowing ball of light shot down the triangular tunnel in twists and turns. Suddenly I exploded out of the tunnel and found myself holding the sword. A dark shape came towards me and I swung the sword at it. The sword passed through the figure but did not cut its physical body. There was no blood. Yet the dark form stopped and started confessing its sins in an unstoppable deluge of evil acts.

Suddenly I opened my eyes and found myself back in the country house staring at a golden sword. I knew the sword was truly magical, I knew what it did but how it worked was still something of a mystery to me. It seemed that the sword had to be made immaterial before it could be used, otherwise you would just cut your opponent open, as with any sword. This sword seemed to cut a person's soul, to cut it open so that it spilled its hidden contents. It was a sword of the soul. But how to make the sword of soul stuff itself?

CHAPTER 23

The children reached the boat and jumped on board and Gideon cast off. He ran to the pilot's seat and started the engine. Within moments they were racing away from the jetty into open sea.

The children stood at the back of the boat watching the helicopters behind them. "There is no way that we can outrun them," said Mythra. "They will catch up to us within minutes. Let's try to teleport out of here. I don't trust Gideon and there is no way this boat can escape those copters."

"Okay," said Tam, "let's try." The children looked around at Gideon. He was in the pilot's cabin. The door to the cabin was closed and Gideon was fixated on driving the boat and so was paying no attention to the children. They breathed deeply and cleared their minds and remembered Michael's house and his lounge. Holding the picture in their minds they began to sing, 'O'.

Suddenly a shrieking high-pitched noise cut through them. The children held their hands to their ears and turned to see Gideon looking back and smiling at them. Tam rushed to the pilot's cabin and tried the door but it was locked. He fished in his pocket for the golden key to open the door. As he pulled the key out of his pocket he saw Gideon pointing at a box on the floor. He opened the box.

Inside the box was a phone. Tam picked the phone up and it rang. He touched the button to answer it. A man's voice said, "There is a film on the phone. Please watch it." The line was suddenly dead. Tam looked at the phone and scrolled through the menu. He found the gallery where pictures and film are stored and found one file. Mythra came close to watch as he clicked on the file and it began to play.

CHAPTER 24

From the Journal of Corvus Raven

I looked at many other objects in the rooms I guarded but had no chance to tune into any as I had with the sword. Whenever I tried, someone would enter the room, people would talk around me and generally I would be distracted in some way or other. One object did catch my interest. A small silver box containing nothing but a very fine powder. It was labelled as being found by Flinders Petrie at Mount Horeb in Egypt.

This I found particularly interesting as I had recently read about the adventures of Mr. Petrie and his inadvertent find. Flinders was a famous archaeologist in the early 1900's and he spent many years studying and searching in Egypt. At one point he decided to re-create the journey of Moses as described in the Book of Exodus in the Bible. Moses led the slaves out of Egypt, across the sea to Mount Horeb where he spoke to God and was given the ten commandments. Flinders followed the route as described and came to a large hill that fit the description of Mount Horeb. He climbed the hill and found upon it a previously unknown Egyptian temple. Inscriptions on the walls of the temple showed that the temple had fallen out of use around the time of Moses. He also found a container filled with a large quantity of fine dust of which Petrie took a large sample. Could this be some of the dust that Flinders Petrie found?

Even more recently I had come across another book which questioned a scene from Exodus. When Moses came down from the Mountain with the Ten Commandments he found the freed slaves had made a golden statue to worship. Moses became very angry as this went against one of the Commandments. However, Moses had not yet given the Commandments to the newly freed slaves so why was he so angry? He then burnt the calf and it turned into a fine powder which he sprinkled into water and then gave this to the freed slaves to drink.

This passage is very odd. If you burn gold it melts into liquid gold, it does not turn into a fine powder. And then why would Moses want his people to ingest this?

However, in the 1990's scientists found that there is a way to burn gold and for it to become dust. It's a complicated and difficult process using electricity but it can be done. The resultant powder is called Ormus or Monatomic Gold. This is gold in its purest form as it cannot be reduced any further by any means. What's more, scientists found that this gold dust has seemingly magical properties. An object coated in this dust can be made to defy gravity and float or to become so heavy that it falls through the earth itself. What's more, objects can seemingly disappear into another dimension altogether. This can be done by the use of heating and cooling or through the use of sound. Could this be the same dust that Petrie found? Could the Egyptians have had this magical powder stored at a secret temple. Could Moses have known about this since he was brought up as a prince of Egypt? Could this be the secret of how the enormous pyramids were built?

Even more importantly, if such a magical dust were eaten, what would it do to the person who ate it?

CHAPTER 25

At first the children weren't sure what they could see on the phone and then they realised that it was the top of someone's head. It was hair. A woman's hair. The camera began to move around the woman and moved away from her so that the children could see more clearly who it was but they had already guessed. "Mom!" gasped Tam.

"Where is she?" asked Mythra.

The film showed their mother, still unconscious, lying on a bed but no-longer in the hospital. A voice, obviously the voice of the person holding the camera, making the film, spoke. It was the same man's voice they had heard moments before over the phone. He said, "We have your mother. We want the book. Gideon will bring you to us. If you co-operate you will see your mother again. If you don't then you will not. Under the seat is a bag. Take it out and put all of your magical items in there, including the Sibylline books and the blue Chintamani control stone that one of you is wearing."

The voice fell silent and the film stopped. The children looked at each other. They knew they had no choice. The game was up. They lifted the seat and found the large hold all sports bag, filling it as instructed.

The children sat down and sighed. They looked back at the three helicopters following behind. There was no escape.

CHAPTER 26

From the Journal of Corvus Raven

For an hour I had to patrol the grounds outside of the house. It was a fairly warm evening for May and the stars shone brightly above me. Large gardens surrounded the house and woodland surrounded the gardens. I walked at the boundary between the gardens and the woods. I tried to stay out of sight and as silent as possible. I couldn't help but wonder if I would see the mysterious woman from the museum.

I had been on patrol for just over half an hour. Every now and then a few of the guests would come out of the house and go for a short walk before re-entering the house. I watched from a distance, unseen in the shadows, hidden amongst the trees. As I watched a couple walk around looking at the stars I felt a tap on my shoulder.

"Come here often?" she asked.

I turned to face her once more. Again, our eyes met and my world seemed to swim about me. All I could say was, "There is something incredibly special about you."

"So, you feel that also?" she asked.

"Yes," I said, "I can barely stand. Being around you is so odd. Why is that? And what is your name?"

"I'm Sophia," she replied, "and as for why we both feel so odd, well, I just think we were meant to meet. We have a past lifetime history together and a future lifetime mystery together. That's what I think anyway. How about you? You're a fairly enlightened chap, what do you think?"

CHAPTER 27

Gideon guided the boat to the nearby island of Hoy. The boat pulled up alongside a jetty where a number of black clad men waited. Behind them the helicopters were landing on a nearby field.

The children had no choice but allow themselves to be herded towards one of the helicopters. They were aware of Gideon carrying the hold all and heading towards one of the other helicopters. One of the black clad men poked Mythra with the nozzle of a gun so as to hurry her up. She climbed aboard the helicopter and sat down and Tam joined her. Within moments the helicopters were up in the air and heading south.

In less than an hour they were coming down to land. They could see the lush greenery of their surroundings as the doors were opened. Again, at gunpoint they were forced to leave the helicopter. They stepped out into bright morning light and began to walk towards what seemed to be an old church.

"This is Rosslyn," said Tam.

"Oh yes, so it is," said Mythra, "We're at Rosslyn chapel; possibly built by Knights Templars and containing carvings of American plants even though it was built before Christopher Columbus set sail for the Americas. This old chapel has always been something of a mystery, hasn't it?"

"Quiet," snapped one of the guards and again Mythra took a poke in the back with the end of the gun.

They entered the chapel and were bewildered by intricate carvings that covered the walls. Tam totally forgot that he was in danger. "Wow, look at this place," he said. "That's the Green Man, the pagan fertility god and these are scenes from the bible and look up at the ceiling, all those five-pointed stars just like in an Egyptian tomb. This isn't a church, it's an initiation centre."

Mythra shushed him but just too late as he too felt a sharp poke in the back.

At one end of the chapel were two great white ornately carved pillars. The children walked up and admired them. Just beyond the pillars they looked at the carvings running along the wall.

"Those carvings are the same as the pictures of the Tarot cards," said Tam.

His musings were suddenly interrupted. To the right-hand side of the pillars there were some steps going down to a doorway. The door opened and a man appeared. "In here," he barked and the guards obeyed, poking and prodding the children towards the steps. They quickly made their way down the steps and through the doorway into another small room set below ground level.

They immediately spotted a stretcher bed against the far wall upon which lay a familiar figure. "Mom," shouted out Tam as he began to rush forward toward her. Guards forcibly held him and his sister back against the wall.

These two guards were not the only occupants of the room. The man who had ordered the guards to come down the steps was also there. He had grey hair and was quite tall and wore a grey suit and white shirt. Next to him stood Gideon. Next to both of them was a table. It was the kind of table that had fold down legs and was obviously only a temporary addition to the room.

On the table sat the hold all sports bag containing the children's magical items and the multi-coloured bag that contained the Sibylline books. Next to that was a device that was obviously an Archimedes clock and next to that was a sonogram and some speakers. The sonogram and speakers were plugged into an extension lead and the wire went out of the door they had entered. This was the only way in or out.

In addition to all of this there were also the two guards that had poked and prodded the children into the room and had followed behind them. This meant that the small room was quite full.

The man with the grey hair spoke to them as he looked through the hold all bag. "So, children I have been looking forward to meeting you," he said. "You have been quite disruptive to my organisation, although I suppose, in the long run, you were nothing more than a slight nuisance. Actually, in the end you have been quite helpful. You have brought me so many goodies. Ah ha," he stated as he pulled something from the bag. He held it up in front of the children. It was the necklace that held the blue stone that Mythra had used to control others. He put the necklace around his neck and held the blue jewel.

"The word of God, the Chintamani stone. How long I have wanted to get my hands on this. I knew your father had it but he was so good at staying hidden. And now you have brought it to me." He stared at the children and then commanded, "Stand with your backs to the wall and remain there without moving, not even a muscle."

Instantly the children stuck to the wall as if magnetized. They were completely frozen. Not even their chest moved in order to breathe. Even though they could not even move their facial muscles, within 30 seconds you could tell that they were starting to panic. After another 30 seconds their eyes started to bulge but this was the only outer sign that they were suffocating and in agony.

CHAPTER 28

From the Journal of Corvus Raven

"I think I need to know who you are and how you did what you did, and why?" said Corvus.

"Why, so you can catch me, report me, have me locked up?" answered the woman.

"No, not at all. I totally agree with what you are doing. In fact, I am only here to do the same thing, to steal magic objects from corrupt, evil people. That is what you're here to do isn't it?" I asked.

"Yep, that pretty much sums it up. We definitely need to talk but not now. You will be needed inside soon. I believe they will want to test your ability to discern magical objects. I'm sure you will impress them, but just make sure you don't tell them everything. See you soon. Don't worry, I'll find you."

And with that she was gone. Then my radio blared into life and I was called inside. I was directed to an upstairs room where I was observed by a few very important people. One of them was called Mr. Friar. Another was called Blackthorne. There was also a psychic present who wore eight rings, one on each finger. Each ring held a different coloured crystal. Instantly I recognised the type of different coloured crystal set in each ring and the person wearing them; it was Topaz. Thankfully she did not recognise me.

They gave me a snake. It was old and dead. In fact, it was ancient. I tuned into it and found myself walking down a tunnel. Someone was whispering a word, over and over again as I walked down the tunnel. It said "layooeesh, layooeesh," again and again.

At the end of the tunnel was a figure in the darkness, a silhouette of blackness with hair that moved of its own accord. In my hand I held a shield. I looked at the shield. It was shiny and new. I could see the dark shape slowly move towards me in the reflection, the hair moving, writhing and hissing.

The figure stepped into a shaft of light and for the first time I saw the face and the head of snakes and the voice whispered layooeesh and then suddenly I was back in my body. For a moment I remembered meeting Sophia in the museum and her joke about being Medusa and I knew the origin and purpose of the snake.

"This snake came from the head of Medusa" I said. "If used correctly it can freeze a man as if he had been turned to stone. However, I don't know how to activate it. Maybe if I had more time to study it I could figure it out." I didn't tell them about the magic words of activation, 'layooeesh'.

Suddenly, an alarm sounded. Everyone looked shocked. A guard entered looking pale. "Sir," he said, "there has been another theft. The Flinders Petrie box has gone, sir."

CHAPTER 29

The grey-haired man laughed at the helpless plight of the children and said, "Okay you can breathe and move your eyes and if I ask you a question you may answer, truthfully."

The children gasped and looked at each other and then looked back to the grey-haired man. He continued, "My name is Blackthorne, Mr. Blackthorne but you can call me 'sir', no, how about 'master'. Yes 'master', that will do just fine. Guards I no longer need you. Wait outside."

The guards left the room immediately. In fact, because Mr. Blackthorne had said 'outside' they left the building altogether and waited in the cool, fresh morning air.

Back inside the small room there was now more space and Mr. Blackthorne walked around as he spoke. "So, do we have all we need for time travel? We have an Archimedes clock, a sonogram and the Sibylline books. Is there anything else I need?"

"A map or a picture of where you want to go," answered both the children in unison.

"Ah yes, of course," said Mr Blackthorne, "this is teleportation as well as time travel. After all, if we just travel in time we will reappear in space. The Earth itself will have moved on to somewhere else. Gideon, the laptop." At his command Gideon took a laptop computer from a small bag on the floor and began to plug it in and turn it on.

"So, children, tell me, actually just one of you tell me. Yes, Mythra, you can tell me. Is this all of the magical items you possess, here in this bag?"

"No," answered Mythra truthfully.

"Oh, so, you have other items, do you?"

"Yes," she answered.

"And where are these items then?" Mr. Blackthorne continued to press.

"In Stourport. In our boat," she answered.

"Ah, yes the boat," repeated Mr. Blackthorne. "Whatever happened to the boat?" he asked.

"It was damaged," Mythra answered. "So, it was taken to a dry dock for repairs."

"And you left your items on board your boat?" He asked surprised. "Are you not worried they will be stolen?"

"They are safe. The boat is safe," she answered.

"So where is this drydock," Blackthorne continued. "Who owns it?"

"It's in Stourport. I can't tell you where exactly but I know how to walk there. It belongs to Michael."

"Michael who?" pressed Blackthorne.

"Ah, Michael. Erm, I don't know his surname," she admitted.

"And you, Tam. Do you know his surname or the name or location of the boatyard?" quizzed Blackthorne.

"No, I didn't ask and I guess I wasn't paying much attention. We were both a bit distracted. Lots going on," said Tam.

"Okay, we will find the boat later," said Blackthorne, realising that he was getting nowhere. "Let's get back to time travel," he said. "Gideon, where and when did you meet these children?"

Gideon told him and Blackthorne said, "Find a map of that location and pictures too. Refresh your memory." As he spoke he opened the multi-coloured bag that contained the Sibylline books. He put his hand in the bag and pulled out what looked like a few sheets of A3 paper. As they appeared the papers glowed with an eerie light. Blackthorne began to flick through the pages. As he turned a page over it seemed to disappear while the number of pages he still had to look through never seemed to diminish.

Somehow only a few pages of the book ever appeared in our dimension at a time.

It took some time but eventually he found the date he was looking for. The page contained diagrams relating to the relative positions of the stars and other writing which appeared to be Egyptian. Blackthorne took some glasses from his pocket and put them on. As he did so he said, "Translation lenses," as he gave the children a quick glance and smiled.

"Ah," he said as he now turned to the Archimedes clock and started to adjust the various cogs from which it was made. As he did so he looked back to the book and then adjusted the clock and so on until he was done. A loud hum suddenly filled the air and then dissipated. Once the clock and the book were at the same setting their harmonisation caused this brief noise.

"That sounds promising," said Blackthorne.

During this whole time Gideon had been staring at the laptop computer. Now Blackthorne spoke to him. "So, Gideon, did you find the map and picture?"

"Yes, master," he answered. "I have been refreshing my memory."

"Good, good," said Blackthorne. "So, I take it you remember everything about where you were when you first met these children?"

"Yes, master," answered Gideon.

"And no doubt you remember how that meeting came about, don't you? You remember why you were there, don't you?" asked Blackthorne.

"No, master," answered Gideon. "Actually, I have no idea why I was there at that time. Nor do I remember where I was before that or anything at all."

"Now isn't that strange," said Blackthorne. "That is funny, isn't it and I have been wondering about that. After all you were our co-operative little captive for quite a while weren't you so you have been questioned quite thoroughly and you really don't know do you? Oh, and in case you are wondering children, yes, we did let

Gideon out for a while to meet you at the museum. We knew you would go for the clock and we figured you would be naïve enough to trust Gideon again, and you did. But where did Gideon come from? Yes, I really had to think about that one. Then I realised. Gideon, what do you have around your right ankle?"

"Nothing, master," said Gideon.

"Can you have a look for me Gideon."

Gideon bent forward and rolled up his trouser leg. Around his ankle was a blue plastic anklet.

"There's nothing there, master," said Gideon.

CHAPTER 30

From the Journal of Corvus Raven

I have had an amazing day with Sophia. As I suspected she had stolen the powder found by Flinders Petrie and she confirmed for me that it did indeed possess the magical properties that I had read about. She also confirmed, as I suspected that this gold dust could be used in conjunction with other objects. For example, this powder could be used to phase the sword of truth into another dimension. The sword could then be used as I had surmised, to cut the very soul of a man so as to pour the truth from him.

When I inquired as to how I could wield a sword that has become immaterial due to its existing in another dimension she hinted at a number of different ways around this problem. Initially she hinted that there may be magical objects that would allow someone to remain here in this dimension whilst wielding the sword. I got the impression that she was referring to some sort of magical gloves. However, when pressed she admitted that it was also possible for a man or woman to slip out of phase from this dimension with the help from monatomic gold.

This explains how she was able to appear to be invisible when I first encountered her but she was not forthcoming as to whether she had ingested the gold or had some other means of accessing this power.

However, I am convinced that she is a powerful psychic who picks up echoes of the future and is able to warp people's senses. I learnt that she used to work for the Nyx and it was in this capacity that she first came across the magical items. It was during this time that she realised that the Nyx were not the benevolent force that they appeared to be. They are not so much concerned with maintaining world order as they are with maintaining their own power over the world order. It was for this reason that she has gone rogue and turned against the organisation.

Very cleverly she has warped the perceptions of those whom she worked with so that her former colleagues either do not recognise her or they see her as some other person. Through this ability she is able to continue to infiltrate their gatherings and gain access to the magical objects. However, she has to be careful as many of those in the higher ranks of the organisation wear protection against this kind of mind warping enchantment. Her strategy relies on the fact that this is a big organisation. Those at the top only know what is going on because those at the bottom report to them. If all the people that know her do not see her as a problem then they will not report her and she can continue to operate incognito.

CHAPTER 31

"Gideon, I order you to be able to see what is around your ankle," said Blackthorne.

"Oh, that," said Gideon, "it's a blue anklet of some sort."

"Here," said Blackthorne, "take these scissors and cut it off."

Gideon did as he was ordered and handed the anklet to Blackthorne. Blackthorne started to twist the anklet and it began to come apart. There was a hollow space inside of it with a small piece of paper in it. He took out the paper and opened it up and showed it to the children. Some numbers were written on the paper. It was today's date.

Blackthorne took another blue anklet from his jacket pocket, along with a pen and a piece of paper. He wrote today's date on the paper and showed the children. It was in exactly the same handwriting. Blackthorne rolled the paper up and put it inside the space in the new anklet and then, kneeling down he fastened the anklet to Gideon's ankle. It clipped together in such a way as to be impossible to take off without cutting it off.

Blackthorne then spoke to Gideon. He said, "You cannot see the anklet that you wear on your right ankle. You do not know it is there and you will not do so until I tell you otherwise. You will not remember any of this, you will not remember me. All you know is that you must meet these children and befriend them and convince them of your mission to destroy the world's computerised money."

Blackthorne then slipped a small computer tablet into Gideon's pocket and said, "Now take this." Gideon took a small jar of powder from Blackthorne and started pouring it into his mouth.

Blackthorne handed Gideon a small bottle of water with which to wash down the powder.

"Now you are ready," said Blackthorne. As he said this he approached the sonogram and turned it on. Once more the children heard the familiar low-pitched hum from the sonogram. Slowly the sound rose to a higher pitch and continued to do so until there was a flash and Gideon was gone.

Blackthorne turned the sonogram off and laughed. "Ha, and now it makes sense. Now I know where Gideon came from and how he first met you and why he had an anklet that he could not see and had no knowledge of. Now I know why he had this foolish idea to destroy computer money. Ha. And do you know what, children?" he asked staring at the children intensely, "Do you know what else didn't make any sense to me? Ha, you'll love this. How did we ever find your father at Fairbourne hall? You see, we didn't know where he was and yet there were our agents destroying his home and instigating this little adventure, this little cat and mouse game that we have played. How on earth did that happen? And now I know how we found you and your poor father and your poor mother. You told us and you gave us the means to go back and burn your home to the ground. Ha ha ha. Don't you see, it was you. Ha ha."

CHAPTER 32

From the Journal of Corvus Raven

September 28 2006

For five years now, I have worked with Sophia, stealing magical items form the Nyx. She is ferociously brave and will not back down. Once she has decided to do something we just have to find a way to do it.

Tonight, was our most dangerous mission of all and our last mission together. We have been tracking the movements of Friar and Blackthorne for some time and we had discovered a secure location where they have some of their most potent magical items hidden.

We entered the building from above. Monatomic gold defies gravity when heated so we have created flying suits which are coated in gold dust and which contain heating and cooling mechanisms. Using this technology, we were able to make ourselves completely immaterial and able to walk through the air at high altitude so avoiding the ground based guards who all wear special goggles and carry specialist weapons able to neutralise our special dust.

When we were directly above the building we were able to activate our cooling circuitry in our suits and descend to the rooftop unseen. I carried with me a steel plate, approximately one metre in diameter. It had a special cooling unit attached and I wore this on my back as if it were an ancient shield. Sophia also wore one as a spare and as a shield in case we were discovered. I placed my disc on the roof top and activated the cooling device by using a remote-control device. Obviously, it was covered in gold dust which, when cooled becomes so heavy it will sink through the earth itself. Very quickly it grew so heavy that it sank through the roof of the building and continued through the floors below that down into the earth.

We entered the building through the hole in the roof directly into the room where we needed to be. Our reconnaissance had paid off. We were in the magical stronghold of Friar and Blackthorne. This fortified room was laden with magic items but there was only one object that we wanted to find; the bag of Orpheus, which contained the Sibylline books, the key to time travel.

It did not take us long to find it despite the fact that it was hidden in an other dimensional cupboard. Using a portable sonogram, we were soon able to open this cupboard and take possession of the bag.

All that remained was to teleport out. We had only practiced this once before and ended up in a tree near to where we had wanted to go but it had worked and we survived so we decided it was the simplest way to get away. We concentrated hard on our location and activated our sonogram.

Suddenly, the door burst open. Friar entered the room holding a sound device which cancelled out our own. We both came out of phase and stood helpless before him.

CHAPTER 33

Suddenly, the laughter stopped and Blackthorne called to the waiting guards but there was no response. "Where are they?" He muttered to himself as he marched to the door. He opened it and called the guards once more and then walked out through the doorway and up the stairs. The guards were nowhere to be seen. Blackthorne huffed and puffed with frustration as he realised his mistake. The guards were all outside. He marched across the hall to the main door and opened it. Seeing the guards stood outside he barked his orders, "You and you, come with me." Together, the three of them marched back to the little underground room.

Blackthorne searched on the computer for a few minutes and then said, "Here, you two, look at this. It's Fairbourne Hall. Memorise the map and these pictures. I want you to think of nothing else."

Blackthorne then moved back to the Sibylline books and started flicking through the pages. "It's alright, he called back to the children, I know the date of the fire. How could I forget? Ah, there it is."

Again, he donned his translation lenses and then fiddled with the Archimedes clock. Again, he referred to the book and again fiddled with the clock until there was a sudden hum that briefly filled the room as clock and book became aligned.

He spoke to the guards who had been obediently memorising the map and pictures of Fairbourne Hall. Blackthorne pointed to one of the pictures and said, "This spot, here at the front of the Hall. I want you to concentrate on this place only. Now take this."

Each guard was given a small vial of powder which they duly swallowed and washed down with some water. Blackthorne approached one of the guards and said, "Here," the guard held out his hand. Blackthorne was holding a small box. He gave it a little shake so the children could hear the rattle of it before placing it in the guard's hand and saying, "You will need these." It was a box of matches.

Immediately, Blackthorne was at the sonogram, starting it up. The low-pitched noise filled the small room. The noise slowly changed in pitch, becoming higher and higher and then a flash and the guards were gone.

Blackthorne turned to face the children laughing like a mad man and then he suddenly stopped and blinked and looked and said, "Where did you get those scarves from? You weren't wearing those before." Suddenly hands reached from the shadows behind him and grabbed him around the face. More hands grabbed his arms as he seemed to be pulled back into the shadows in the corner of the room.

A voice said, "Now."

The two children jumped forward to the sonogram and reset it. The voice said, "Here," and the children saw two small vials being handed to them from the darkened corner of the room. They swallowed the powder inside and started the machine. The hum filled the room. Within moments there was a flash and they were gone.

CHAPTER 34

From the Journal of Corvus Raven

Friar reached out for Sophia meaning to rip the Orphic bag from her shoulders but as she twisted he accidentally grabbed the steel shield which ripped away from her shoulders far easier than he had expected. He staggered backwards and fell with the shield lying on his chest. From his pocket he pulled out a gun. It was aimed at Sophia. He was about to fire.

I couldn't have allowed that at any time but now that she was pregnant I acted as a man possessed. I pressed the button on the remote control that operated the cooling device on the steel plate and almost instantly friar was crushed through the floor and carried down into the earth by the metal plate.

We were too distraught to teleport so we activated the warming units in our suits and floated rapidly into the night sky. As we did so we activated the sonograms in our suits in order to become immaterial just as gunshots rang out, passing through the space we had physically occupied only moments before.

Finally, our mission is ended. We have taken all we can take from the Nyx. Now we have to make sure these items stay hidden from them, just as we have to stay hidden from them, not just for our sake but for the sake of the unborn twins that my wife carries.

Our journey is over. Their journey into the world of magic and enlightenment is about to begin. After all, with us as their parents, what choice will they have?

CHAPTER 35

For the children everything became colours and lights in a dizzying, dazzling kaleidoscope. Suddenly nothing was solid. Time seemed to stop and then just as suddenly they could feel the ground beneath their feet. It took a few more seconds before they could begin to see as they were still blind from the colours and lights in their heads. Slowly they began to see shapes. They both staggered, feeling dizzy as if they had been spinning on the spot. Then they felt the cool air on their faces and began to perceive darkness. It was night time. They were stood up and they were outside.

A large shape loomed before them and they heard a groan and something that sounded like a man falling on to gravel. The large shape began to become more solid and detailed. It was a building. They were stood in front of a building. It was their home, Fairbourne hall. It was their home before the fire.

Again, they heard groans. They looked down. Two men lay on the floor by their feet. They looked to be in some pain or discomfort. In truth they were dizzy and disorientated. Time travel had not agreed with them. As the Archimedes clock and Sibylline books had been set for the same time all four of them had arrived in the past at the same moment despite the fact that the guards had gone first. However, these guards were not prepared for the trauma of time travel. Unlike the children they had not been to the Great Pyramid and prepared for this in the etheric box of the Atlanteans.

However, the children felt wonderful and were just realising this. They felt empowered and full of energy. Looking down at the two guards Tam said, "Mythra, do you see these coloured lights around these men? That's their aura isn't it?"

"Yes, I see it too," said Mythra. "In fact, you should see your aura, Tam. It's like a multicoloured Phoenix. You look amazing."

Tam took a good look at his sister for the first time and saw the same effect surrounding her. "Yes, that's how you look too, he said. Is this enlightenment?" He asked.

"Yes, it is," answered Mythra staring at her own hand and the flaming light surrounding it, "and yet it's not as well. I can't explain but I guess this a stage of enlightenment. There is further we can go. We can be more enlightened than this in time but this is enough for now."

"Yes, your right," said Tam, "but I feel that we don't need those magic items anymore, that any powers they may have given us, we now have within ourselves."

"Yes, Tam," agreed Mythra. "I have this sense of just knowing this is true, just as if I were wearing that golden woolly hat."

"Yes, and I know I could see hidden magical objects now without the green lenses to help," added Tam.

As the children spoke the two black clad guards had staggered to their feet and started to look around. As one, Mythra and Tam both reached out a hand and said, "Stay."

The guards froze to the spot, seemingly frozen in time itself.

Just then the children heard a click and turned towards the front door of Fairbourne Hall. They both knew that the sound was the door opening and they both knew who would emerge. The door opened and before them, stood in the doorway was their father.

He started to walk out towards them as they began to run to him. They all clashed together in a huge hug. After a few moments he pushed his children back and asked, "What are you two doing out here? Let me look at you. There is something different about you. What is it? What's going on here?"

"We think we have become enlightened, father," answered Mythra.

"It's a long story, Dad," said Tam, "but we have travelled back in time to save you and mom from these two men. They came here to burn Fairbourne Hall and kill you and put Mother into a coma and in the process of all of that we have become enlightened, sort of anyway."

"This is some story," said their father, "and yet I sense the truth in your words. What's more I just checked your room and saw you both in bed, pretending to be asleep, probably because you intend to go for a midnight snack."

"Yes," said Mythra, "that's exactly what we are going to do and while we do that the fire will start and we will lose everything, or we would have but now we don't need to, you're safe, mom is safe, our home is safe."

"Hmm, well you need to tell me more," said their father.

Hurriedly, Mythra and Tam told of their adventures since Fairbourne Hall had burnt down. They told of their escape on the boat, finding magical items, meeting Gideon, being chased by the Nyx, teleporting, meeting Michael, collecting the items for time travel having being tricked into doing so by Gideon and being captured by Mr. Blackthorne.

"And you say someone helped you escape?" asked their Father.

"Yes," answered Mythra, "but we didn't see who it was, they must have been invisible in some way. They put our scarves around our necks and that freed us from the spell we were under. We were no longer controlled by the word of God stone. Somehow, they held Blackthorne while hiding in the shadows, as if they were part of the shadows. And they gave us the gold powder to take before coming here."

"They?" asked their father.

"Yes, there was definitely two of them," answered Tam.

"And you can't guess who they were?" asked their father.

The children looked at each other and a sudden realisation came across them both in a flash. Together they both said in unison, "It was us!"

"We freed us!" said Mythra.

"Yes," said Tam, "our younger selves are getting up now and creeping in to the kitchen and soon they will be on the run and we will be here in the background, helping us without our knowing."

"Yes," said Mythra, "we make sure Michael is around to meet us and we call him to make sure he lets us go to the television transmission station."

"And we make sure the Nyx know where we will be when we go to Orkney and we have to make sure that gate in the Great Pyramid is open," said Tam.

"And then we are there to save us and make sure we can get back here to stop these two from burning down our home," said Mythra.

"Is that really true though?" asked Mr. Raven.

"What do you mean?" asked Mythra.

"Well, children, if there is no fire you will not go on the run and you will not have this adventure and so you will not become enlightened and you will not be standing before me right now. So there has to be a fire, doesn't there?" Their father looked at them in all seriousness and with utter conviction and the children knew he was right.

"But you die!" said Tam.

"Was my body found?" asked Mr. Raven.

"No," answered the children.

"So, then I don't have to die. I just need to keep out of the way for a while."

"But what about Mom?" asked Mythra.

"Yes," said Mr. Raven, "that is a bit trickier but I can put your mother into a trance spell, a sleeping beauty spell she once used on me, so that she appears to be in a coma and I can fully protect her from the effects of the fire with magical items. It's not a great thing to do but I don't see that we have any choice. If we make any changes then you won't get to this moment now and you have to get to this moment now in this state of enlightenment. We have no choice. I take it that apart from the coma, that your mother is fine, isn't she? In the future she is safe with you two. And if the coma is a magically induced one then you can wake her and she will be perfectly okay. I know it's awful to steal a few months of her life like this but we have to get to this moment now otherwise reality itself may fall apart."

The children were not happy about this but understood that there was no other option.

"We are running out of time," said their father. "I need to prepare your mother. You two need to wake these guards. Order them to continue their mission to burn down the Hall. Do you remember seeing these two when you escaped the fire?"

"Yes, but we saw them from the boat house. They went down to the water and got into a boat there," said Mythra.

"Once they have lit the fire then they need to wait for you two, well the other you two, to get to the boat house. Once you or rather they are at the boat house then lead them down to the river where they will find a small boat with an outboard motor in which they can escape and report to the Nyx. Oh, and don't forget to tell them to forget all about seeing you right now. Oh, and tell them to go into hiding, otherwise there will be two of each of these chaps turning up at work and that will confuse everything. Okay? He asked, are we ready to go?"

The children hugged him with tears in their eyes. "Father," said Tam, "can't you come with us?"

"Perhaps I could but if my body is not found the Nyx will be using all of their resources to find me. It's probably best if I stay away from you two for a while. Come on kids, he said, keep it together, everything is going to be fine, in fact you already know what's going to happen next so do as little as possible while keeping the story on track. Okay, let's go, he said as he gave them one last squeeze and then turned and ran indoors."

Reluctantly, Mythra ordered the Guards to follow their previous orders and set fire to the Hall. The children even showed them where they could find some petrol to help get the fire going. Despite their feelings of guilt for doing this they knew their father was right. The fire needed to happen, they needed to have the adventure.

Once the fire was burning brightly the children ordered the guards to wait until they were signalled by the children. Mythra and Tam walked down to the river bank where they found the small boat described by their Father. They looked down the river toward the boat house in the distance and waited until they saw their younger selves down there. It wasn't long before they saw themselves in the distance. Both of the children realised that they could zoom in as if they were looking through binoculars and that seeing in darkness was no problem for them at all.

Seeing their own past selves was as strange as anything they had experienced since the fire.

Once they were sure that it was the right time they called to the guards who immediately began to run towards them at the river bank. Mythra and Tam knew that at this moment a younger Mythra and Tam were looking back towards the house and seeing these scary shadowy shapes move towards the river.

Sirens blared and Tam and Mythra remembered that it was at this time that the fire engines turned up. They knew there was nothing else to do but to give these two guards their final instructions. Inform the Nyx that they had found the Ravens house and destroyed it and then go into hiding for a few months.

CHAPTER 36

Mythra and Tam continued to watch over their younger selves over the next few months. On the morning that they met Gideon down by the river they found him first. He appeared from the future before them on the river bank as they waited for him. He was completely confused as to where he was and what he was supposed to do so they calmed him down and gave him his orders.

They realised that Gideon was stuck in a time loop forever going around in circles and always coming back to this time and place and living the same bit of story over and over again. They realised that this was too much of a punishment even for Gideon. They decided that as soon as they were able they would find a way to free him from this loop without destroying the story that they needed to protect.

The children stood and watched, hidden by trees and bushes as Gideon approached their boat, the Hermes. They saw Tam on deck looking up and down the river even though he and the boat were invisible.

As Tam looked at his past self he remembered something from this day, something he had seen down the tow path; a teenager talking with some children. His head span and he grabbed hold of Mythra. "Look," he said.

Further down the towpath they could clearly see the children and the teenager just as Tam had remembered. Mythra looked and at first did not realise what she was seeing but within moments the realisation dawned and her jaw dropped. "Oh my... I don't believe it that's us, with Gideon!" she said in utter shock.

"Yes, that's right," said Tam, "It made no sense to me at first but everything is starting to fall into place for me. This is the Gideon we met originally, before Blackthorne got hold of him and put that anklet on him."

A spark of understanding came to Mythra's eyes. "So," she continued, "we meet this Gideon, have some adventure, he gets captured by Blackthorne and sent back to meet us. So, the time we remember meeting Gideon was actually the second time we had met him. We had already been through this story once before."

"Yes," said Tam, "look at us on the boat right now, we're meeting Gideon again. But to us, to our younger selves, we are meeting him for the first time. That's the nature of the time loop. The very first time we met Gideon has been overwritten by his travelling back in time so we do not remember that adventure, its as if it never happened."

"And in the future," continued Mythra, "we choose to travel back in time to meet this original Gideon and save him from being stuck in this time loop."

"Yes," said Tam. "In a way there are now two Gideon's. The one we are meeting at the boat who is destined to be stuck in this time loop forever and this younger Gideon who we save from ever taking part in this adventure."

"I wonder what our future selves are saying to him right now?" pondered Mythra.

"Well, I have a pretty good idea what I would be saying to him, don't you?" asked Tam. "Do you remember, Mythra, what you said about him burning down his own house, possibly killing his own father?"

"Yes, Tam," Mythra replied. "So, we would be talking to him about redemption, about making things right, about some role he can play, some change he can make within himself."

"Yes, Mythra, I believe that's right," responded Tam.

CHAPTER 37

The children continued to work in the shadows, making sure that all the pieces fell neatly into place. They called Michael and told him that he needed to go out on his boat early on the morning that he found them. They called him again to make sure he allowed them to go on the mission to the television transmission station. They also appeared to Gideon in his cell and persuaded him to co-operate with his captors so that he could help them in the Museum when they stole the Archimedes clock.

They shadowed themselves in the Great Pyramid, making sure the gate was unlocked to the descending passageway and making the noises that distracted the guards. Finally, they informed the Nyx that their younger selves would be on the Orkneys and then they waited at Rosslyn chapel for the final showdown with Mr. Blackthorne.

Once Blackthorne had left the children to fetch the guards they entered the room in a state of invisibility. The last thing they wanted to do was shock and confuse their younger selves at this moment so they used the scarves, which protected against magic spells and the voice of God, to free the children and then used their enlightened powers to hide in the shadows.

Once the younger Mythra and Tam had disappeared in a flash of time travel they were able to step out and show themselves to Mr. Blackthorne.

He gasped when he saw them, "B-but how?" He stuttered. "I just saw you go…"

"Yes, Mr. Blackthorne, you just saw us go where?" asked Mythra.

"B-back in time," he answered.

"Yes, that's right, we went back in time, to make sure your terrible plot failed and obviously it did," said Mythra as she walked over to her mother, still unconscious on her bed, and gave her a gentle kiss.

"It's funny thinking about it though Mythra," said Tam, "we were worried about Gideon in his time loop but I only just realised that in a way we are also in a time loop. There are two of us that always reach this point and go back in time and yet there are two of us, that's us, who are now free to continue to live our lives."

"Oh, yes, Tam, that's sooo confusing but I suppose you are right," agreed Mythra.

At that moment the other two guards came into the room. "Is everything alright sir?" the one asked without fully taking in the situation inside the room. Suddenly the guards realised that all was not as it should be and they went to raise their weapons but Mythra and Tam were too fast for them. Both of them raised their hands and said, "Stay."

Both the guards froze as if hit by a time bomb. Mythra then ordered the guards to sit in a corner and to forget all they had seen and heard. As she finished giving her orders they heard a voice outside the door say, "Hey is there any room for me in there?" The voice was followed by a friendly face poking through the doorway.

"Dad!" Both the children shouted. Their father entered and they all hugged. Finally, they were all back together again.

"How very touching," they heard from behind them. They span to look and there was Blackthorne with a gun raised and pointed at them. "Think you are fast enough to stop me from shooting you, do you? Do you want to try?" He asked.

The children and their father stood transfixed. Could they stop him? Could they freeze him fast enough to stop him from firing? Could they freeze time and stop a speeding bullet if he fired right now?

These questions raced through the childrens' minds and then

suddenly there was a loud thump and Blackthorne fell forward, slumped to the floor in an unconscious heap. Behind him stood the children's mother shaking her right hand and rubbing her bruised knuckles. "You will not threaten my children," she said as the children rushed towards her with tears in their eyes and they all held each other. Corvus Raven joined his family and said, "It's lucky you gave your mom a kiss to wake her from the sleeping beauty spell." He smiled and put his arms around his family. Finally, their nightmare was over. Or so they thought.

The door suddenly burst open as a hurricane wind blew through the small room. The whole family was pushed back against the far wall hardly able to breathe as a chill wind cut through them. The table overturned and threw itself and its contents at them. The wind was so fierce they could hardly open their eyes to see the cause of this onslaught. Frozen water became mixed in with this unnatural gale, slicing and piercing the skin as the family were held breathless and in pain against the wall.

Corvus Raven forced his eyes open just enough see the figure stepping through the doorway, a figure with a different coloured ring on each finger.

"It's Topaz," he screamed at the top of his voice to make himself heard above the noise of the howling winds.

"I am amazed you remember me, Mr. security guard," Topaz cackled as she sent more and more ice and wind screeching and slashing and slicing into the family who were utterly defenceless. The children were unable to think, unable to concentrate and so unable to protect themselves or their parents.

In desperation Corvus called out as loud as he could as ice shards slashed at his face, "I knew you before then," he cried, "In the Himalayas."

"What?" screeched a shocked Topaz. For a brief moment the storm abated as Topaz took this information in but before anyone could react Topaz screamed, "No." As she screamed the force of the wind and ice increased to an even greater ferocity, matching the anger of Topaz herself. The Raven family once more found themselves being cut by thousands of fragments of ice as they were pinned to the wall. The whole family began to scream with agony.

Suddenly a figure flew through the doorway and crashed into the back of Topaz sending her tumbling forward. The figure landed on top of topaz and tried to hold her still.

Corvus Raven looked at this figure trying to remember where he had seen him before. "I know you," he said, "you look younger but it is you, the man from the tea shop in Nepal; the man who gave me directions to the sacred hidden valley."

Tam and Mythra were trying to recover their senses after taking an elemental battering. They heard their father's words and looked at the figure on the back of Topaz in shocked realisation; it was Gideon.

Both of the children instantly understood what needed to be done. "Mom, Dad, get out of here now," shouted Mythra.

As her parents ran for the only exit, Topaz shrugged off the young figure of Gideon. She pointed at him with the ring holding the purple Topaz crystal and a wind instantly threw Gideon back against a wall.

Mythra held out a hand and shouted, "Stay," and for a brief moment Topaz froze but then shrugged off the magical attack. She pointed all of her fingers at Mythra and unleashed an elemental onslaught of wind, water, ice and fire but this time Mythra was ready. She held out her hands and the ferocious elements parted in front of her. An invisible shield, a bubble of energy protected her and her brother who had been on the floor behind her the whole time, finding the right page in the book, setting the clock and now starting the sonogram.

"Ready," Tam shouted as the tone began to rise.

"Help me," shouted Mythra.

Tam stood and held out his hands mirroring his sister. They looked at each other and with a slight smile shouted as one,

"Now." They both pushed with all of their might and their bubble of protection expanded and knocked Topaz backwards towards Gideon. Both of the children leaped forward, grabbing hold of both Gideon and Topaz as the noise of the sonogram rose.

Suddenly there was a flash and all four figures disappeared.

Corvus and Sophia Raven stood outside of Rosslyn, nervously waiting for their children to come through door. They both ran when ordered, without thinking about it but now they wondered if they had done the right thing. Panic began to rise within them and they felt the urgent need to run back into the building. Silence had descended and moments seemed to drag out into minutes.

"Corvus, we have to go back in," said Sophia in desperation.

"Okay," answered Corvus, "let me go first."

They both approached the doorway as a flash of light shone behind them. They both turned to see the light diminish and the forms of their children appear before them.

Once more the Raven family were reunited with hugs and tears. "Your master sends his regards," said Mythra as her parents relaxed their hold enough to allow the children to talk.

"So, you have been to the hidden valley?" asked Corvus.

"Yes, we were there for a few weeks actually," said Tam, "We had to tell your master all about you, after all we were there a few years before you."

"Yes, that boy, Gideon was it, he was the one who met me in Nepal, who told me where to find the valley," said Corvus.

"We heard you say that when you saw him and then we knew what to do with him and Topaz," said Mythra. "Hopefully Gideon will find some salvation there. At least he serves a useful purpose in your story as well as ours now."

"And you came back without the clock and the book?" asked Sophia.

"Yes, father's master helped us with that," said Tam. "Come on we need to find Blackthorne."

The family entered Rosslyn chapel and entered the small room at the bottom of the stairs. Inside was a sodden mess. Corvus immediately made his way to the Sibylline books and retrieved it from the flooded floor. Sophia and the children found the soggy, unconscious form of Blackthorne lying in the water, still unconscious from the blow from Sophia and oblivious to the elemental storm that had transpired only minutes before.

When Mr. Blackthorne awoke he was ordered to forget the Raven family and everything that had happened. The helicopter pilots who had been waiting with their machines were also ordered to forget the family and their trip to the Orkneys. All of the guards, pilots and Mr. Blackthorne were ordered to visit the police and admit to any and all crimes they had ever committed. Once this was all done they walked away from Rosslyn towards the nearby carpark. A large black vehicle sat waiting. As they approached the car the side door slid open and Michaels friendly face appeared. "I received a phone-call saying I should be here. Anyone need a lift," he asked.

"Actually," said Mythra, "I feel like going on an adventure. How about you Tam?"

"I don't think we should," he said smiling.

Printed in Great Britain
by Amazon